A New Friend

by Paul Webb
illustrated by Roberto Fino

Harcourt
SCHOOL PUBLISHERS

ISBN 10: 0-15-351301-2
ISBN 13: 978-0-15-351301-5

Ordering Options
ISBN 10: 0-15-351211-3 (Grade 1 Advanced Collection)
ISBN 13: 978-0-15-351211-7 (Grade 1 Advanced Collection)
ISBN 10: 0-15-358029-1 (package of 5)
ISBN 13: 978-0-15-358029-1 (package of 5)

2 3 4 5 6 7 8 9 10   179   15 14 13 12 11 10 09 08 07

There was a noise from on top of the barn. The cow wanted to see what it was, but the barn was too tall.

Pig trotted across the yard.

Cow said, "Please stand on my back to see what is on top of the barn."

3

The barn was still too tall, and Pig could not see.

Dog came past.

"Dog, could you please stand on my back?" asked Pig.

The barn was still too tall, and Dog could not see.

Dog called, "Bird, please come and join us. Could you fly up and see what is on top of the barn?"

Bird was surprised. "There is a little kitten stuck on top of the barn!" said Bird. "She is all by herself."

"Oh, my!" said Cow. "That kitten needs some help. Please tell her we will help."

Kitten jumped onto Dog's back and joined the animals in the yard.

"There is always room for a new friend," they said to Kitten.

"Thank you for being so nice," Kitten purred.